Read Alone

Pinocchio

Level 6

9-10 years

1100+ Words

A long time ago there was a kind old puppet maker named Geppetto.

He lived all alone with a cat and a goldfish.

"I am very lonely," he felt one day. "It's raining and I have no one to talk to."

That night, he made a puppet for himself. He called the puppet Pinocchio.

The puppet looked like a real boy. “Ah!” said Geppetto, “Oh how I wish he was my son!”

This wish came to the Blue Fairy's ears. That night, she flew to Geppetto's house. She gently touched Pinocchio with her magic wand.

Pinocchio blinked his eyes as he came alive. "Am I alive?" he yawned and asked.

"You are alive. But not a real boy yet. If you are good to Geppetto, then you will become a real boy, made of flesh and bones", said the Blue Fairy to him.

Just then, a little cricket peeped out of a box. The fairy said, "Cricket will always help you and keep you out of trouble."

Then poof! The Blue Fairy disappeared.

In the morning when the puppet maker saw Pinocchio, he jumped for joy.

"Oh my, I can't believe my eyes!" he cried, "I have a son! I have a son!"

Geppetto bought his little wooden son everything a little boy needed. He bought him warm clothes and books for school.

Now, Pinocchio thought that school was boring. So he didn't like it. But Cricket warned him, "All right then. Don't go to school. Become a silly boy."

"No," said Pinocchio, "I don't want to become silly. I'll go to school and learn very fast. Then I can work and earn lots of money for Pa."

And then he happily set out for school.

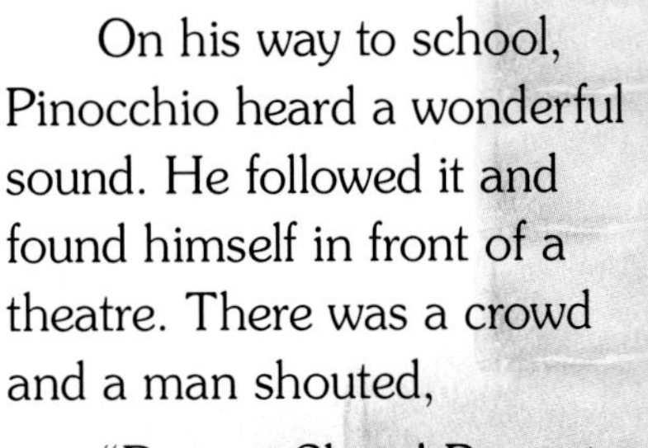

On his way to school, Pinocchio heard a wonderful sound. He followed it and found himself in front of a theatre. There was a crowd and a man shouted,

"Puppet Show! Puppet Show! Come on in and enjoy the dance!"

"What fun!" thought Pinocchio. He forgot about school and sold all his books to buy a ticket.

Inside, the puppeteer saw Pinocchio "Ah!" he thought, "A puppet with no strings! Wait till I have him in my show. I'll be rich!"

So the puppeteer caught hold of Pinocchio and threw him into a room with the other puppets. Poor Pinocchio began weeping.

"I'll never ever see Pa again!" he cried, "Who'll earn money for him when I'm not there?"

This reached the puppeteer's ears. He began missing his own father. Then he felt sad for Pinocchio and let him go. What's more, he even gave Pinocchio five gold coins for Geppetto.

"Go straight home to your father," said the puppeteer to Pinocchio, "And next time, go to school!"

"Yes, sir," said Pinocchio.

When Pinocchio was hopping home, he started playing with the gold coins. He thought, "Aha! What if I turn these five coins to fifty? I'll be rich, rich, rich! Then Pa will be so proud of me!"

Meanwhile, a lame fox and a blind cat were hiding behind a fence and heard this. Their greedy eyes shone when they saw the gold coins.

Then they leapt up from behind the fence and stood before Pinocchio. "Hello kid!" the fox said. "We're just the right people for you. Now let's see what you have. Hmm...Five gold coins! Bury them in this magic snow. You'll find a tree full of gold coins when you come back."

"Just do it!" said the cat.

Pinocchio buried his coins and returned to the same place. But he found no tree. And no gold coins either. The lame fox and the blind cat had stolen his coins!

Pinocchio stared at the ground in anger. Cricket told him, "You should be careful when you trust someone."

"Out of my sight, you silly cricket!" he screamed at Cricket. And he cried all the way till he reached home.

That night, the Blue Fairy appeared to Pinocchio.

"Good evening, Pinocchio," she said in a sweet voice, "Did you go to school today?"

"Yes I did. And I studied so much." And his nose grew long.

"Where are your books?" the Fairy asked.

"They're at school with the teacher," Pinocchio answered. This time, his nose shot out like a tree branch. "Why is my nose growing so long? I don't like this," he exclaimed.

"A lie always grows, my child, just like your nose," said the Blue Fairy, "From now on, your nose will grow each time you tell a lie. When you tell the truth, it will shrink."

"I promise I will tell the truth," Pinocchio told the Blue Fairy.

Then Blue Fairy told him that while he was away, his old father went searching for him. And now he was lost at sea.

Pinocchio put his hands on his cheeks and cried, "It's all my fault! I must leave once and find him!"

Pinocchio and Cricket reached the edge of the sea but couldn't go any further. A wild storm was raging and huge waves crashed against the shore.

"Let's wait until the storm gets over," Pinocchio told Cricket, "Then we can take a boat and look for Pa."

Right then, a wagon came by, with a peddler and lots of boys and girls in it. They were laughing and joking and singing.

"Come with us to Toyland," they called, "Where everyone plays and there is no end to fun!"

"What if it's a trick?" warned Cricket, "Please don't go."

"You worry too much, Cricket," replied Pinocchio, "I'll only be gone for a short while. The storm would be over by then."

And off he went to Toyland.

Pinocchio was really enjoying himself in Toyland. There was music and there were games and candies.

Suddenly, Pinocchio looked into a mirror and found that his ears had grown very long. They looked like a donkey's ears!

Poor Pinocchio was very scared.

The peddler had given him magic food to turn him into a donkey. He ran after Pinocchio shouting, "Ha! Ha! Now you will pull my wagon for me!"

Pinocchio ran as fast as he could. He could feel his tail growing.

"No!" he cried, "I want to be a real boy! Not a donkey!"

"Jump into the sea!" cried Cricket, "Quick!"

Pinocchio leapt into the sea. In the water, he became himself again. But soon a giant whale came and swallowed him whole.

Pinocchio rolled and he tumbled into the whale's belly. And there, to his surprise, he found his father!

"Pa!" he cried. His father hugged him tightly and said, "I searched so hard for you. At last, you are here!"

Pinocchio had an idea to escape from the belly of the whale. He found a feather on his father's table and tickled the whale. The whale sneezed so hard that they flew right onto the beach!

When Pinocchio and his father were back home, his father asked him, “”What happened to your nose?”

Then Pinocchio told him the truth about the bad things that had happened to him. “I have been a very bad boy Pa,” he said. The moment he said this, his nose grew short again.

Just then, the Blue Fairy appeared. She told Pinocchio, “You have learned your lesson at last. I have a little surprise for you.”

She gently touched Pinocchio with her magic wand. Pinocchio could feel his skin become soft.

“I’m a real boy!” he cried and danced with Cricket and Pa, “I can pinch myself!”

And they all lived happily after that, and Pinocchio’s old father was never lonely again.

Head Words

puppeteer, peddler, yawned,
warned, earn, weeping, theatre,
leapt, trick, exclaimed

Questions

1. Why did Pinocchio's nose grow?
2. Why did the peddler want to turn Pinocchio into donkey?

Read Alone

Alice in Wonderland

Level 6
9-10 years
1100+ Words

It was a hot summer day. Alice was sitting beside her sister under a tree. When Alice peeped into the book her sister was reading, she thought,

"And what is the use of a book without pictures?"

The heat made Alice feel very sleepy. She was just about to sleep, when through the corner of her eye, she saw a White Rabbit, dressed like a proper gentleman, walking hurriedly. He pulled out a watch from his pocket and said, "Oh dear! Oh dear! I shall be too late!" and walked even faster.

At this, Alice burned with curiosity and darted after the rabbit.

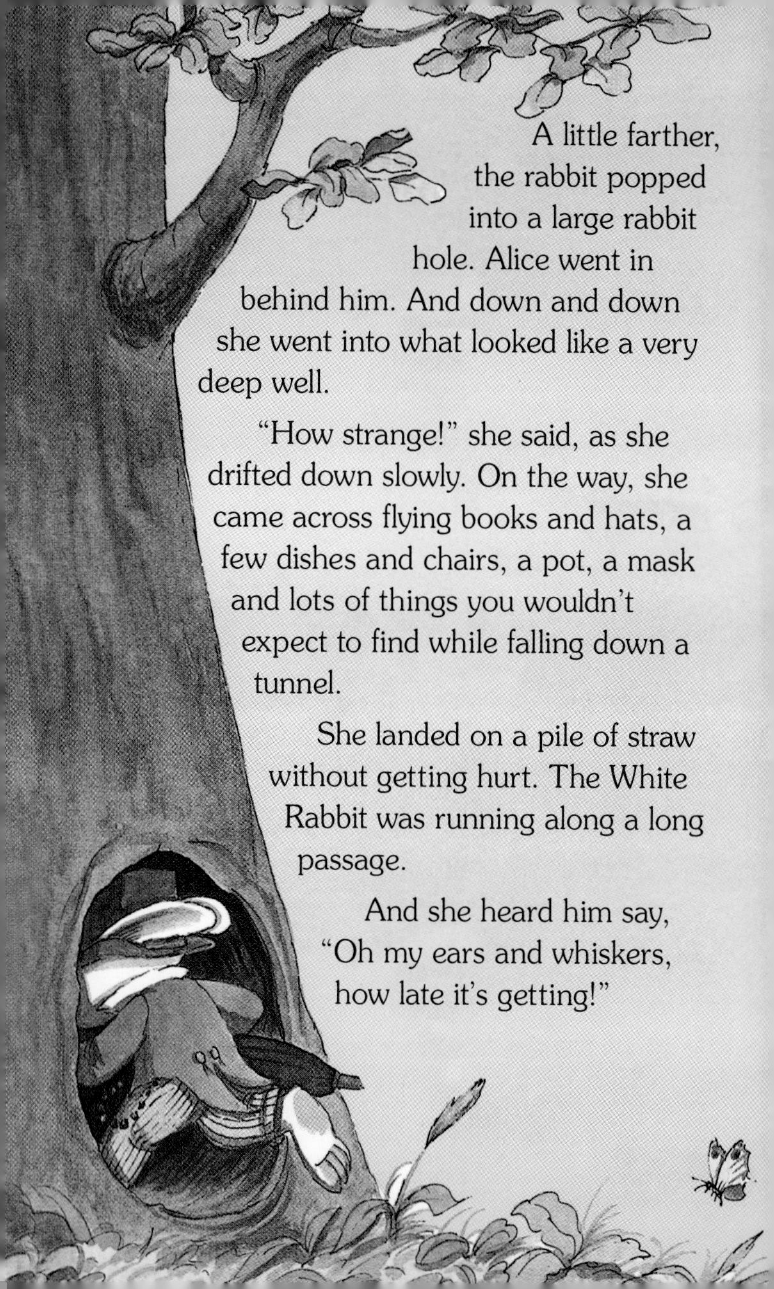

A little farther, the rabbit popped into a large rabbit hole. Alice went in behind him. And down and down she went into what looked like a very deep well.

"How strange!" she said, as she drifted down slowly. On the way, she came across flying books and hats, a few dishes and chairs, a pot, a mask and lots of things you wouldn't expect to find while falling down a tunnel.

She landed on a pile of straw without getting hurt. The White Rabbit was running along a long passage.

And she heard him say, "Oh my ears and whiskers, how late it's getting!"

Alice quickly ran behind him and when she turned a corner, found herself in a large hall lined with doors.

Each of them was locked. Suddenly she came upon a table, with a tiny golden key on it. With it, she tried to open all the doors. It finally opened a small one hidden behind a curtain. Beyond it, she saw the loveliest white roses in a garden. But the door was too small for Alice.

"How I wish I could fold up like a telescope!" she said. And right in front of her she noticed a bottle she hadn't seen before. It had a note which said "Drink me".

When she drank it, she shrank into just the right size for her to fit through the door. But she had left the key on the table! She tried climbing the table, but it was too high for her. So she sat on the floor and cried.

And right on the floor, there was in front of her a dish of cookies. Next to it was a note that said, "Eat Me." So she ate a little bit of the a cookie.

Now Alice found that her head had hit the ceiling and her feet were very far off from her. She had grown very tall. So she started crying again. This time, her tears were so big that they made a river inside the hall. Alice shrunk again because of the water. And when she became only a few inches tall, she was carried with the flow through the keyhole of a door.

On the other side, she saw the White Rabbit again, hurrying towards her, still muttering, "I'm late! I'm late."

When the White Rabbit reached Alice, he poked her and asked, "What are you doing here Mary Ann? Go fetch my white gloves from my house right now. Quick!"

Alice rushed to the White Rabbit's house, even though she knew she wasn't Mary Ann. She picked up the gloves from the bedroom upstairs. Just when she was about to leave, she found a little bottle next to the mirror.

"I'm tired of being tiny," she said, "Let's see what happens if I drink from this bottle." And when she drank, she grew so large that her poor head got stuck inside the house and her hands and legs stuck out from the windows!

When the White Rabbit reached home, he saw Alice and thought she was a monster. So he started throwing pebbles at her. But when they hit her cheeks, Alice felt that they were rather soft. It turned out that the pebbles had turned into cakes!

She had two cakes and she became smaller than she ever was. "Oh dear!" exclaimed Alice, "When will I ever be my right size again?"

"Here, have a mushroom," said a caterpillar with a feathered hat, stylishly. "One side makes you taller and the other makes you smaller." So Alice had both sides until she became herself again. "Now, I wonder where the White Rabbit went?" A Cheshire Cat perched on top of a tree said, "With the Queen, darling, at the croquet match. I'll see you there." And she vanished into thin air, leaving behind only a grin.

A little ahead, Alice came upon a large table, all ready for tea. Around the table sat the March Hare, the Mad Hatter and the Dormouse.

"No room! No room!" they cried when they saw Alice coming.

"Not at all," said Alice, "look, there's plenty of room." Alice sat down comfortably on the couch as she was hungry. The March Hare dipped his watch into the tea, the Mad Hatter spoke gibberish and the Dormouse kept falling asleep while telling stories. They were all rude to her. So Alice was indignant and left.

Alice really wanted to find the White Rabbit now. Soon, she reached the garden with the lovely white roses. Three playing-card men were busy painting the roses red.

"Would you please tell me," she asked," why are you painting those roses?"

"You see, ma'am," they replied politely, "that if the queen sees white roses here instead of red, she will be quite cross and will have our heads chopped off."

The next moment, the Queen of Hearts and her court arrived. The playing cards bowed to her. But Alice wasn't sure whether such things are done at processions. So she just stood in her place.

"What girl is this who dares not to bow to me?" shouted the Queen.

"My name is Alice, if you please, Your Majesty."

"Can you play croquet?" shouted the Queen.

"Yes!" Alice shouted back.

"Then don't just stand there! Follow me!" cried the Queen. And off marched Alice behind the Queen.

"How very curious!" exclaimed Alice when she saw the croquet game. There were live hedgehogs for balls and the mallets were live flamingos. Throughout the game the queen kept shouting, "Off with their heads!" every time she was losing.

At one point, the Cheshire Cat appeared in a tree. "How're you doing, darling?" she mewed to Alice.

"I think the Queen cheats. I really don't like her!"

"Off with her head!" screamed the Queen, who happened to be right behind Alice.

"What rubbish!" protested Alice. Just then, a loud voice was heard announcing, "The court is in session. The trial starts now!"

"To the courts! To the courts everyone!" the Queen ordered everyone.

At the court the Queen sat down sternly on the judge's seat. "Read out the charges," she commanded.

The White Rabbit unrolled a scroll and read,

"The Queen of Hearts, she made some tarts
    All on a summer day:
The Knave of Hearts he stole those tarts

And took them quite away!"

"Where's the first witness?" bellowed the Queen.

And Alice was quite surprised and shocked when the White Rabbit pointed out to her and said, "There! Alice is the first witness."

Alice walked up to the Queen and stood before her.

"What do you know about this business?" said the Queen.

"Nothing," said Alice.

"Nothing whatever?" asked the Queen.

"Nothing whatever," said Alice. "This is all nonsense." "Hold your tongue," said the Queen, turning purple.

"I won't," said Alice.

"Off with her head!" shouted the Queen at the top of her voice.

And Alice was surrounded by the playing-card soldiers at once.

"Who cares for you?" said Alice. "You're nothing but a pack of cards!"

At this, the whole pack rose up in the air and swooped towards her. She gave a little scream, half in fright and half in anger. She swung her arms left and right and tried to beat off the cards. She also heard the Cheshire Cat behind her, laughing and saying, "How're you doing, darling?"

And Alice felt as if she was falling deeper and deeper, with the cards constantly shuffling around her.

Alice found herself lying on her sister's lap. Her sister was gently brushing off some of the leaves that had drifted down from the trees upon face.

"Wake up, Alice dear!" said her sister. "Why, what a long sleep you've had!"

"Oh, it was such a curious dream," said Alice. She told her sister all the strange adventures she had under the rabbit hole.

"That was really a strange dream you had Alice," her sister told her. "But now run in for your tea dear. It's getting late."

And Alice got up and ran home. But on the way, she didn't notice the White Rabbit again, who was watching her from a hole in the tree. He put back his watch in his waistcoat and hopped away.

Head Words

darted, drifted, muttering, stylishly
couch, gibberish, indignantly,
charges, bellowed, shuffling

Questions

1. Why did Alice get angry with the March Hare, the Mad Hatter and the Dormouse?
2. What was so strange about the croquet game?

Read Alone

Peter Pan

Level 6
9-10 years
1100+ Words

Wendy, Michael and John lived with their parents in London. Every night, Wendy would read out stories to her brothers.

From all the stories they heard, the character they loved best was a boy named Peter Pan. He lived among fairies and when children died, Peter was with them.

Now their mother too knew lots of tales about Peter Pan. When she heard Wendy telling the boys about Peter, she said, "He must have grown up by now."

"Not at all Mum," said Wendy "Peter will never grow up. He'll always be my size."

Just then, mother saw a few leaves on the floor and wondered where they came from.

"Ah!" exclaimed Wendy, "Peter's at it again!"

That night, when the children were going to sleep, they saw a light flickering in their room. When it came to a standstill, they saw a little fairy, no larger than their little finger. It was Tinker Bell, one of Peter Pan's friends. Right then, Peter dropped in.

"Where on earth is my shadow?" he asked Tinker Bell.

"Over there," said Tinker Bell.

Peter leapt up to catch his shadow and tried to merge with it, like two drops of water would merge. But the shadow kept slipping from his fingers or just ran away. Finally, Peter gave up and sat down on the floor and cried.

Wendy got up and asked Peter where he lived. Peter replied,

"Second to the right, and straight on till morning."

Wendy observed that it was a very funny address indeed.

"I'm serious," said Peter.

"Is that what they write on your letters?" asked Wendy.

"Don't get any letters," Peter said.

"Doesn't your mother get letters?"

"Don't have a mother," he said.

"Is that why you're crying," Wendy asked.

Then Peter said that that wasn't the reason. He told her about the shadow.

So Wendy stitched back the shadow onto Peter. Peter asked the children if they would all like to go to Neverland, the land where lost boys live.

"I'll teach you how to jump onto the wind's back!" he told them.

Peter blew fairy dust on them. And off they flew to Neverland.

"Whee!" shouted Michael.

"Wait till you see the mermaids and pirates in Neverland," said Peter.

"Let's go quickly!" exclaimed John.

And they soared high up into the night sky until they could see a dot in the distance.

"The island!" said the children together.

Peter pointed to a pirate ship in the distance and told them about a pirate called Captain Hook. "He has a hook where his right hand should be and he claws with it," said Peter.

"Claws?" asked John, scared.

Peter then explained how Hook got it. "A large crocodile once bit off his hand. It's still hungry for the rest of him. After that, the crocodile swallowed his clock. So every time Hook hears the ticking of a clock, he turns pale with fear."

Now Tinker Bell began to get jealous of Peter being so friendly with Wendy. She flew down to a group of the lost boys who were hunting.

"You see that huge bird there? Peter wants you to shoot it," she told them. One of the boys took careful aim at Wendy and shot. It struck her and she came floating down with an arrow in her chest.

Peter swooped down to catch her. When he had caught her, he landed slowly and laid her on the ground.

Peter Pan was furious at the lost boys. He was about to punish them, when Wendy stirred. The arrow had merely lodged on a button. Wendy was safe!

Then Peter introduced his friends to them. "Meet Wendy, Michael and John," he said.

"Hello Wendy, Michael and John!" shouted the boys, "Welcome to Neverland!"

After that the children stayed underground, where the lost boys lived. Every night, Wendy tucked them into bed, told them stories and sang to them.

During the day, they would all play pretend games in a place called Slightly Gulch. And every day they would have a new imagined adventure.

And now it was time for a real adventure.

One day, the children saw Captain Hook. He had kidnapped a girl called Tiger Lily. Peter went to Hook and fought with all his might to set her free. Twice he was clawed by the iron hand. But he finally got past Hook, caught hold of Tiger Lily and flew off with her.

Soon it was time for Wendy and her brothers to go back home. Tinker Bell had been ordered by Peter to lead the way.

But as they were leaving, Captain Hook launched a fierce attack. In the battle that followed, Wendy and the boys were taken as captives and taken back to the pirate ship. Peter managed to escape and went back home. There he fell into a deep, dreamless sleep.

Peter didn't know that Captain Hook had followed him. When Captain Hook saw that Peter was asleep, he added five drops of poison to Peter's cup.

Peter woke up and lifted up his cup to drink.

"Don't drink it!" shrieked Tinker Bell, "It's poisoned!" And Tinker Bell flew between the cup and Peter's lips and swallowed the drink. Her wings began to quiver and she could not fly anymore.

"It's time for me to die," said Tinker Bell, "But I might live if children believed in fairies again."

"If you believe in fairies," shouted Peter, "then wink twice. Don't let Tink die."

And guess what happened? Tinker Bell fluttered her wings again!

Back in the pirate ship, Wendy had been tied to the mast and the boys were about to be thrown into the sea. The pirates were pointing their swords at each of them.

"I'll count to three," said Captain Hook to the boys, "and then you'll all have to jump. Or else..."

"One...two..."

And then he heard the tick-tock of the crocodile. He went silent and began to shudder. The sound drew nearer and nearer.

Captain Hook ran frantically around the ship, looking for a place to hide. Obviously, he had no idea that it was Peter who was making the noise.

But the tick-tocking slowly stopped. Captain Hook gathered whatever courage he had left and shouted, "Fling them all overboard!"

"Ha!" said one of the pirates, "No one can save you all now."

"You are just so wrong, my friend!" shouted Peter Pan and swung at the pirate. The next moment, this pirate was on the ground and Captain Hook charged at him.

"So, James Hook," said Peter, "We meet again."

"But for the very last time," said Hook and leapt forward. But Peter was swift and agile. He matched every stroke of the sword with Hook. And Peter dodged every thrust of Hook's sword.

Then Hook started swaying his sword wildly. At one point, Hook turned around and Peter gave him a powerful kick. Captain Hook went flying overboard right into the mouth of the crocodile who was waiting for him.

As for the rest of the pirates, they started running in all directions.

"Go get them," Peter called out.

The pirates were so scared and confused that most of them jumped off the ship. The others hid in dark corners. But when they were found out, they too leapt into the sea.

Back home in London, the children's parents were very worried. Peter didn't want the children to go back home. So he told Tinker Bell to shut the window to their room, so that Wendy would think that her mother has barred her out and doesn't love her anymore.

But just then Peter saw the children's mother crying. So he opened the window and let the children fly in.

The children were tired but very excited after having such an adventure.

"Stay with us please Peter," said the children, "and go to school with us too! We'll have lots of fun."

"Go to school?" said Peter, "and grow up into a man? Nobody's going to turn me into one." Saying this, Peter flew back into the boundless night sky with his arms spread out.

Head Words

character, flickering, standstill, observed, lodged, pretend, fluttering, mast, frantically, nimbly

Questions

1. Why did Peter Pan cry?
2. What was Captain Hook scared of and why?

Read Alone

The Steadfast Tin Soldier

Level 6

9-10 years

1100+ Words

There were once twenty five tin soldiers who were all brothers, crafted out of old tin spoons. All of them looked the same, except for one. This soldier had one leg missing because there was not enough tin left to complete him. But like the others, he too shouldered his gun, looked straight ahead, and wore a smart red and blue uniform.

The first time the soldiers saw the light of day was when the lid was taken off the box. And the first thing they saw and heard was a little boy clapping his hands and crying, “Soldiers! Soldiers!”

He lined them up in front of his toy castle, so that they would guard it and also protect the princess.

The boy placed a beautiful paper doll near the gate of the castle – she was to be the princess. She wore a white lace dress with a blue ribbon over her shoulder. And how graceful she was! She was a ballerina and danced on one leg, with the other leg gracefully raised high. So the tin soldier thought that like himself, she only had one leg.

"She would be perfect as my wife," he thought, "but she is a princess and I am merely a soldier. She belongs to a castle, but I only have a small toy box to live in and twenty five of us share it." And so he looked at the princess and just smiled at her.

That night, the toys came out to play, as they did every night. The tin soldier had hid himself behind a snuff box so that he wouldn't have to be in the toy box with his brothers. He waited eagerly to meet the ballerina.

From his hiding place, he saw the nutcracker do his somersaults, sticks of chalk scribbling on the slate, the stuffed cat chasing the wind-up bird and the toy train chugging around the room. And finally, he saw the princess dancing on one leg and smiling a little smile at him.

When the clock struck twelve, out flew the lid of the snuff box and pop! A jack-in-the box sprang towards the tin soldier.

He was a mean and angry crow. But the soldier stood there, bravely facing him.

"Listen, why don't you keep your eyes to yourself?" he yelled, "And not on her. She's mine, you hear!"

The tin soldier held his ground.

"Oh, high and mighty, eh? How dare you ignore me?" screeched the crow, "You just wait and see what happens to you."

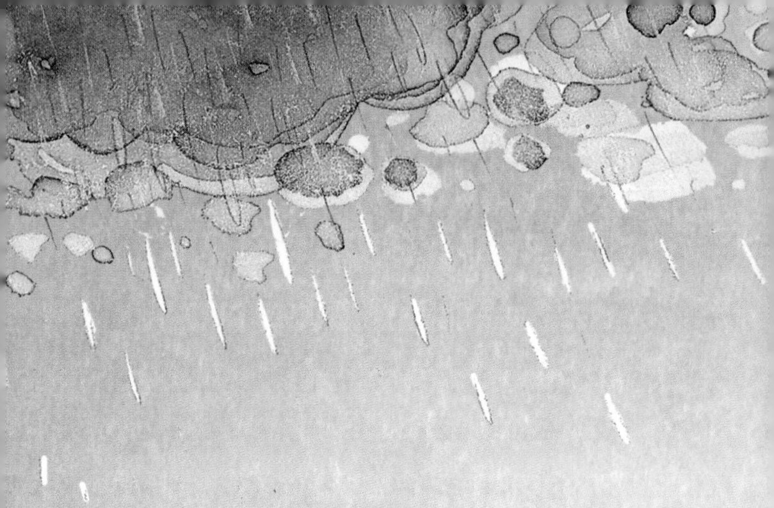

The next morning, while playing, the little boy put the tin soldier on the window sill. Now it might have been a gust of wind or the evil crow. But something pushed the tin soldier very hard and he flew headlong into the street outside. And his bayonet got fixed between two cobblestones.

The boy rushed downstairs to find the soldier, but it began to rain quite hard. So he couldn't go outside.

There lay the tin soldier. Outside. Outside in the rain.

After it stopped raining, two boys saw the tin soldier and picked him up. One of them said, "Let's make a paper boat and put him in it. Then we'll sail it on the flooded street."

"Whee!" they said excitedly as they watched the tin soldier sail. And he sailed along the gutter down into the dark sewers.

The current was very swift and the soldier's boat could have drowned at any moment. The soldier shuddered, but he stood steadfast with his gun on his shoulder, without looking down even once.

"If only the princess was here," he thought, "then even if it was twice as dark, it wouldn't have mattered."

Then the current became even faster, because he had come to a roaring waterfall. And further down the sewer he went.

In this tunnel, a wild water rat came up to him and said, "Do you have a pass? What! He doesn't have one! Don't let him through." And he chased the tin soldier.

But the steadfast tin soldier held his musket even tighter. And the raging current took him even further.

He sailed for a while and then he saw a light up ahead. His heart grew hopeful, for it finally looked like a way out of the dark tunnel.

But when his boat neared the light, it swirled and was pulled from all sides. And the tin soldier slipped into the water and was immediately swallowed by a fish.

It was slimy and darker than before in the belly of the fish. This time, the tin soldier was courageous as always and stood straight and tall.

Just when he was about to balance himself, the fish began to sway wildly. It finally stopped, and after a while, a flash like lightning fell upon the tin soldier's eyes. He was once more in broad daylight. After which, he saw much excitement around him.

"He's actually travelled in the belly of a fish!" they said, "How wonderful!"

And guess where he was? In the same house he was in before, with the same children and with the very same toys he had been with.

"He's been such a brave soldier. I will honour him by making him stand next to the princess so he can be her special bodyguard," said the boy.

So the tin soldier stood next to the lovely paper doll he loved and said to himself, "I am going to protect the castle and my princess with my life. It will be such a joy to be close to the woman I love."

Just then, without any warning, and for no reason at all, one of the boys picked up the soldier and threw him into the fire.

The tin soldier was now in the fire, melting. He shouldered his gun even more firmly than before and still managed to stand straight and tall. He gazed into the eyes of the maiden he loved and she looked at him.

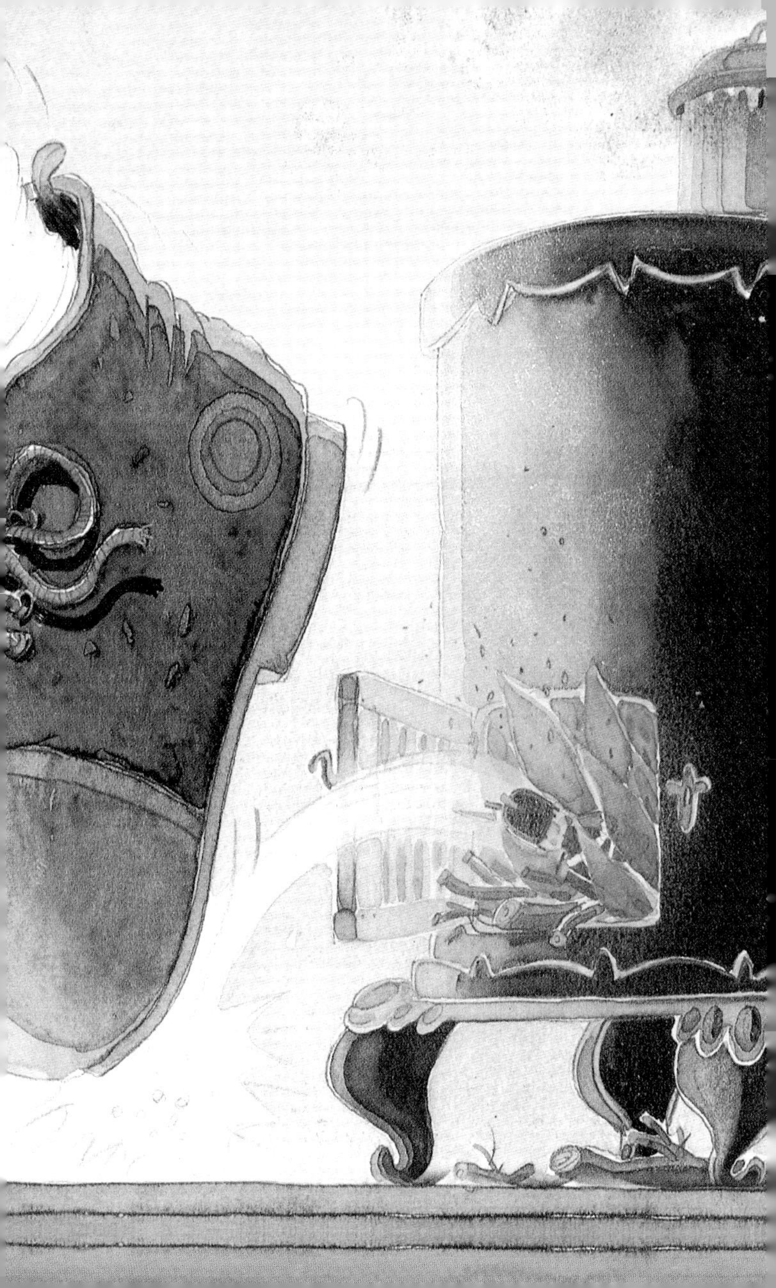

Then a door suddenly opened and the little dancer was lifted by the incoming wind. She flew right into the fire next to the soldier. They were together at last.

All night long the fire blazed. It should have been enough to leave no trace of the steadfast tin soldier or the princess. Or was it?

Early next morning, when the maid was taking out the ashes from the stove, she discovered a small tin heart and a tiny shred of a blue ribbon. She was so surprised that she took them to the toy-maker.

Who knows, but the toy-maker might just have made another ballerina doll. And perhaps another tin soldier, this time with two legs instead of one.

Head Words

crafted, merely, nutcracker, somersaults,
eagerly, headlong, bayonet

Questions

1. What made the tin soldier think that the princess had only one leg?
2. Why is the one-legged tin soldier called "the steadfast tin soldier"?